This Book
Belongs To:

....

....

Beatrix Potter™

Peter Rabbit's Christmas Collection

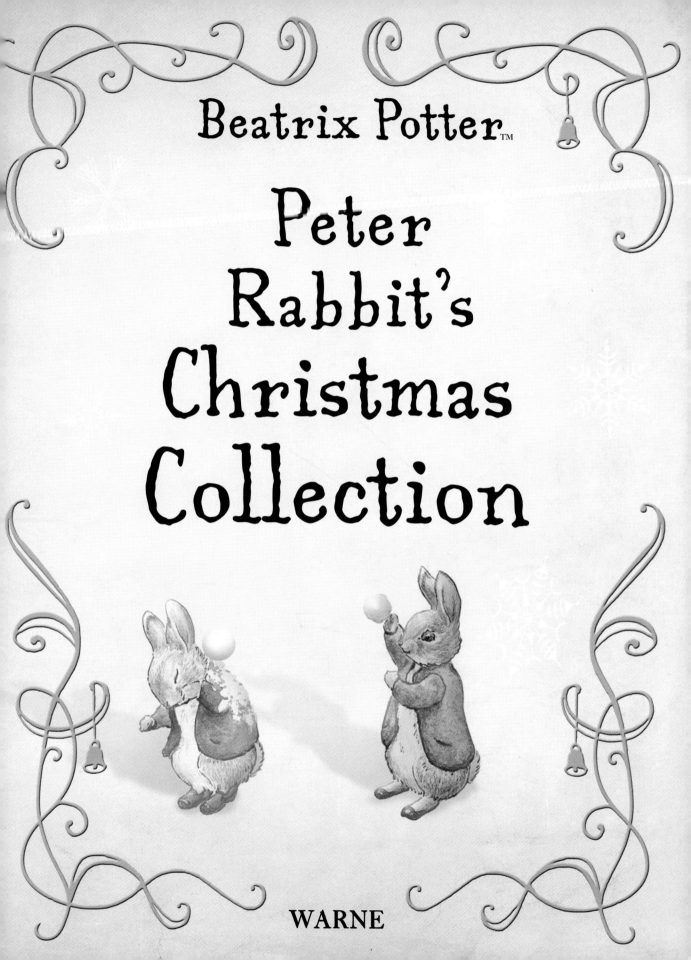

WARNE

FREDERICK WARNE

Published by the Penguin Group
Penguin Books Ltd, 80 Strand, London WC2R 0RL, England
Penguin Group (USA) Inc., 375 Hudson Street, New York, New York 10014, USA
Penguin Group (Canada), 90 Eglinton Avenue East, Suite 700, Toronto, Ontario,
Canada M4P 2Y3 (a division of Pearson Penguin Canada Inc.)
Penguin Ireland, 25 St Stephen's Green, Dublin 2, Ireland (a division of Penguin Books Ltd)
Penguin Group (Australia), 707 Collins Street, Melbourne, Victoria 3008, Australia
(a division of Pearson Australia Group Pty Ltd)
Penguin Books India Pvt Ltd, 11 Community Centre, Panchsheel Park, New Delhi – 110 017, India
Penguin Group (NZ), 67 Apollo Drive, Rosedale, Auckland 0632, New Zealand
(a division of Pearson New Zealand Ltd)
Penguin Books (South Africa) (Pty) Ltd, Block D, Rosebank Office Park,
181 Jan Smuts Avenue, Parktown North, Gauteng 2193, South Africa

Penguin Books Ltd, Registered Offices: 80 Strand, London WC2R 0RL, England

www.peterrabbit.com

First published by Frederick Warne 2014

001

The 'Rabbit Postman' image on p. 25 used courtesy of Major Tom Smith
The 'Bunnies in the Snow' images on p. 82 used courtesy of the Rare Book Department,
Free Library of Phliadelphia

New reproductions of Beatrix Potter's book illustrations copyright © Frederick Warne & Co., 2002
Frederick Warne & Co. is the owner of all rights, copyrights and trademarks in the
Beatrix Potter character names and illustrations.

ISBN 978-0-14135-350-0

Printed and bound in China

CONTENTS

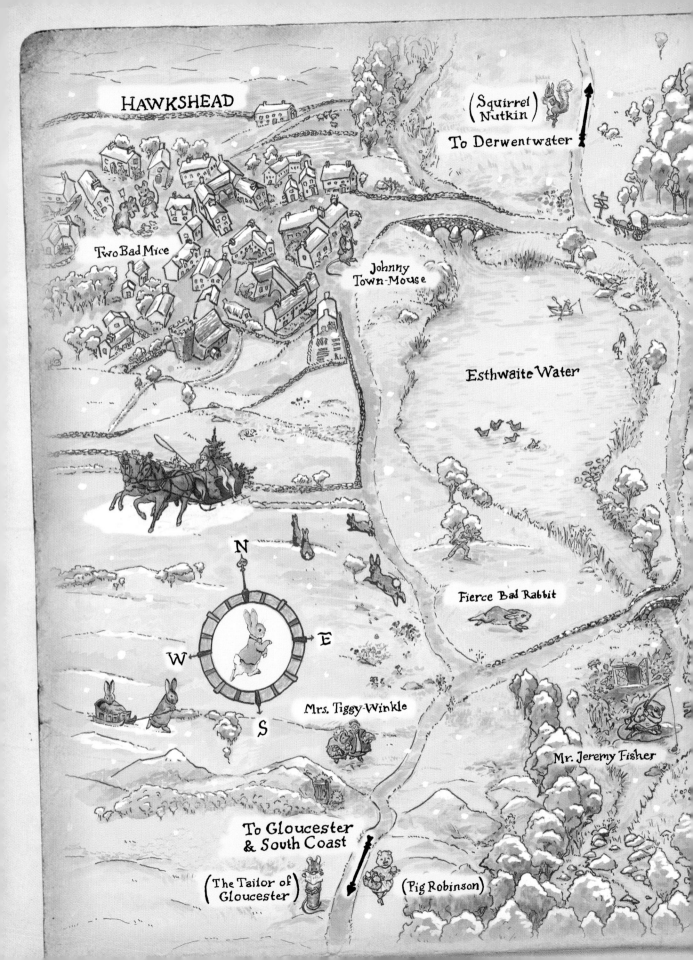

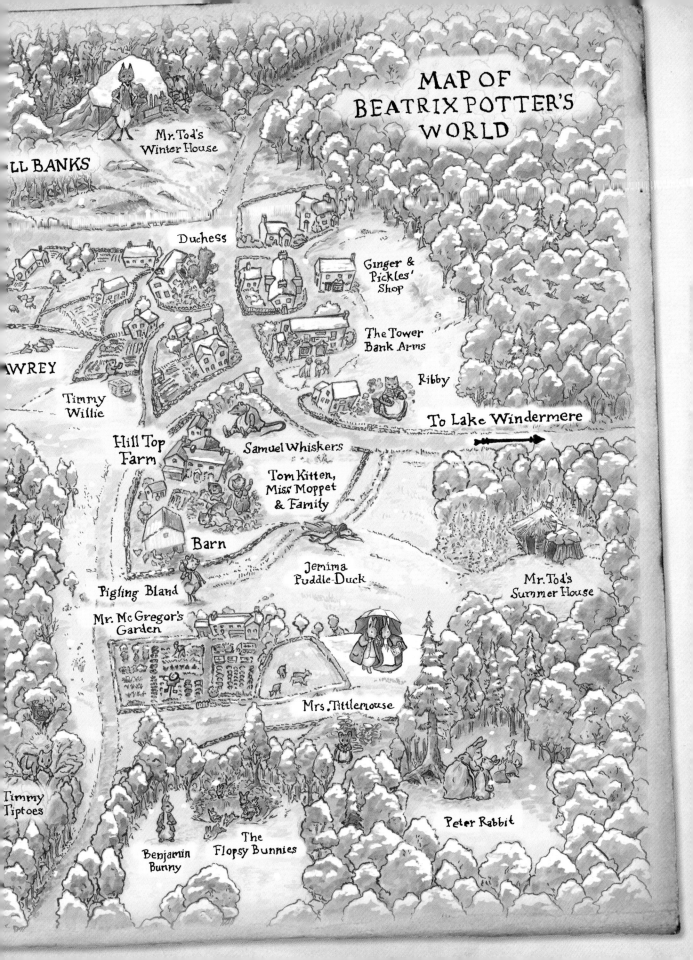

MAP OF
BEATRIX POTTER'S
WORLD

LL BANKS

Mr. Tod's
Winter House

Duchess

Ginger &
Pickles'
Shop

The Tower
Bank Arms

WREY

Ribby

To Lake Windermere

Timmy
Willie

Hill Top
Farm

Samuel Whiskers

Tom Kitten,
Miss Moppet
& Family

Barn

Jemima
Puddle-Duck

Mr. Tod's
Summer House

Pigling Bland

Mr. McGregor's
Garden

Mrs. Tittlemouse

Timmy
Tiptoes

Peter Rabbit

Benjamin
Bunny

The
Flopsy
Bunnies

ABOUT BEATRIX POTTER

Beatrix Potter was born in London in 1866 and spent her first Christmases in a Victorian house in Bolton Gardens, Kensington, with her family and her pets. Christmas must have been very important to Beatrix when she was a little girl as she returned to the festive season time and again in her work.

In 1893, Beatrix Potter sent an illustrated letter to her friend's five-year-old son, Noel Moore, which described the adventures of a rabbit called Peter who sneaked into Mr. McGregor's garden. This story was to become *The Tale of Peter Rabbit* and has been enjoyed by generations of children since its first publication in 1902. Beatrix never lost sight of her most important readers and sent many more picture letters featuring Peter and his friends to children all around the world.

Many of these picture letters were written at Christmas, to bring extra festive cheer to her fans. Beatrix wrote letters from her characters – Peter Rabbit and Benjamin Bunny describe decorating their big fir tree; the Flopsy Bunnies list what they would eat for their Christmas dinners – and would post them in Christmas cards featuring her own exquisite artwork.

Beatrix Potter had always designed Christmas cards for her family and, in 1890, she began to sell them to the stationery firm Hildesheiner & Faulkner, a practice she continued for many years. Beatrix's designs frequently featured animals, often familiar characters from her *Tales*, and a selection can be seen in this book, some for the first time since the late nineteenth and early twentieth centuries.

THE TALE OF
PETER RABBIT

ABOUT THIS BOOK

The story of mischievous Peter Rabbit in Mr. McGregor's garden first appeared in a picture letter Beatrix Potter wrote to Noel Moore, the young son of her former governess, in 1893. Encouraged by her success in having some greetings card designs published, Beatrix remembered the letter seven years later, and expanded it into a little picture book, with black-and-white illustrations. It was rejected by several publishers, so Beatrix had it printed herself, to give to family and friends, before it was finally published by Frederick Warne in 1902.

Beatrix had more in store for the little rabbit in the blue coat. Peter made reappearances in other of her *Tales* and frequently appeared on her Christmas cards and letters.

ONCE UPON A TIME there were four little Rabbits, and their names were —

> Flopsy,
> Mopsy,
> Cotton-tail,
> and Peter.

They lived with their Mother in a sand-bank, underneath the root of a very big fir-tree.

"Now, my dears," said old Mrs. Rabbit one morning, "you may go into the fields or down the lane, but don't go into Mr. McGregor's garden.

"Your Father had an accident there; he was put in a pie by Mrs. McGregor.

"Now run along, and don't get into mischief. I am going out."

Then old Mrs. Rabbit took a basket and her umbrella, and went through the wood to the baker's. She bought a loaf of brown bread and five currant buns.

Flopsy, Mopsy and Cotton-tail, who were good little bunnies, went down the lane to gather blackberries;

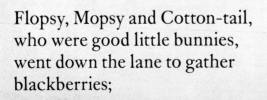

But Peter, who was very naughty, ran straight away to Mr. McGregor's garden,

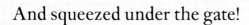

And squeezed under the gate!

First he ate some lettuces and some French beans; and then he ate some radishes;

And then, feeling rather sick, he went to look for some parsley.

But round the end of a cucumber frame, whom should he meet but Mr. McGregor!

Mr. McGregor was on his hands and knees planting out young cabbages, but he jumped up and ran after Peter, waving a rake and calling out, "Stop thief!"

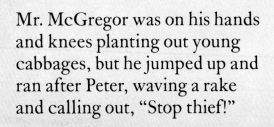

Peter was most dreadfully frightened; he rushed all over the garden, for he had forgotten the way back to the gate. He lost one of his shoes among the cabbages,

And the other shoe amongst the potatoes.

After losing them, he ran on four legs and went faster, so that I think he might have got away altogether if he had not unfortunately run into a gooseberry net, and got caught by the large buttons on his jacket. It was a blue jacket with brass buttons, quite new.

Peter gave himself up for lost, and shed big tears; but his sobs were overheard by some friendly sparrows, who flew to him in great excitement, and implored him to exert himself.

Mr. McGregor came up with a sieve, which he intended to pop upon the top of Peter; but Peter wriggled out just in time, leaving his jacket behind him,

And rushed into the tool-shed, and jumped into a can. It would have been a beautiful thing to hide in, if it had not had so much water in it.

Mr. McGregor was quite sure that Peter was somewhere in the tool-shed, perhaps hidden underneath a flower-pot. He began to turn them over carefully, looking under each.

Presently Peter sneezed — "Kertyschoo!" Mr. McGregor was after him in no time,

And tried to put his foot upon Peter, who jumped out of a window, upsetting three plants. The window was too small for Mr. McGregor, and he was tired of running after Peter. He went back to his work.

Peter sat down to rest; he was out of breath and trembling with fright, and he had not the least idea which way to go. Also he was very damp with sitting in that can.

After a time he began to wander about, going lippity — lippity — not very fast, and looking all round.

He found a door in a wall; but it was locked, and there was no room for a fat little rabbit to squeeze underneath.

An old mouse was running in and out over the stone doorstep, carrying peas and beans to her family in the wood. Peter asked her the way to the gate, but she had such a large pea in her mouth that she could not answer. She only shook her head at him. Peter began to cry.

Then he tried to find his way straight across the garden, but he became more and more puzzled. Presently, he came to a pond where Mr. McGregor filled his water-cans. A white cat was staring at some goldfish; she sat very, very still, but now and then the tip of her tail twitched as if it were alive. Peter thought it best to go away without speaking to her; he had heard about cats from his cousin, little Benjamin Bunny.

He went back towards the
tool-shed, but suddenly, quite
close to him, he heard the noise
of a hoe — scr-r-ritch, scratch,
scratch, scritch. Peter scuttered
underneath the bushes.

But presently, as nothing happened,
he came out, and climbed upon
a wheelbarrow, and peeped over.
The first thing he saw was
Mr. McGregor hoeing onions.
His back was turned towards Peter,
and beyond him was the gate!

Peter got down very quietly off
the wheelbarrow, and started
running as fast as he could go,
along a straight walk behind
some black-currant bushes.

Mr. McGregor caught sight of
him at the corner, but Peter did
not care. He slipped underneath
the gate, and was safe at last in
the wood outside the garden.

Mr. McGregor hung up the little jacket and the shoes for a scarecrow to frighten the blackbirds.

Peter never stopped running or looked behind him till he got home to the big fir-tree.

He was so tired that he flopped down upon the nice soft sand on the floor of the rabbit-hole, and shut his eyes. His mother was busy cooking; she wondered what he had done with his clothes. It was the second little jacket and pair of shoes that Peter had lost in a fortnight!

I am sorry to say that Peter was not very well during the evening.

His mother put him to bed, and made some camomile tea; and she gave a dose of it to Peter!

"One table-spoonful to be taken at bed-time."

But Flopsy, Mopsy, and Cotton-tail had bread and milk and blackberries for supper.

The End

Christmas Deliveries

The joy given by a beautifully written Christmas card cannot be underestimated. Rabbits especially appreciate them, as Beatrix Potter illustrated in this festive card.

Rabbits also love to give and receive presents. Food and rabbit tobacco (or, as humans call it, lavender) are especially popular.

Greetings

Here, Beatrix Potter illustrated Benjamin Bunny delivering a basket of parcels as a Christmas card.

DEMERARA SUGAR

from

The Fairy Caravan

'Hill Top Farm at Night' by Beatrix Potter (15th December 1912)

ABOUT THIS BOOK

This wonderfully Christmassy story is taken from Beatrix Potter's only novella. First published in 1929, *The Fairy Caravan* was written for older children. It is the story of an extraordinary travelling circus of animals. In this chapter excerpt, 'Demerara Sugar' is a tale told by the chicken Selina Pickacorn and her friends. It is a story which begins with a funny misunderstanding and very nearly ends in disaster. Unusually for Beatrix Potter, this story features humans and, luckily for our chicken friends, two human boys save them from an otherwise unsavoury end. The story features an exquisite Christmas party, with animals dancing around a fir tree 'all tipped with light, and wreathed with icicles and chains of frost.' This image clearly had resonance with Beatrix Potter who, as you will see at the end of this story, also illustrated the image in a Christmas card.

UPON FINE DAYS IN SPRING the parrot's cage was set out of doors upon top of the garden wall, opposite the farmhouse windows. In the intervals of biting its perch and swinging wrong-side up, the parrot addressed remarks to the poultry in the yard below. The words which it uttered most frequently in the hearing of those innocent birds were, 'Demerara sugar! demerara sug! dem, dem, dem, Pretty Polly!' The chickens listened attentively.

When the chickens were feathered, they were taken to live in a wooden hut on wheels in the stubble field. They picked up the scattered grain; and grew into fine fat pullets. In autumn the farmer talked of taking the hen-hut home. But he was busy with other work; he delayed till winter.

In the night before Christmas Eve there came a fall of snow. When Tappie-tourie looked out next morning the ground was white. She drew back into the hut in consternation. Then Selina Pickacorn and Chucky-doddie looked out. None of them had ever seen snow before; they were April hatched pullets without a single experienced old hen to advise them.

'Is it a tablecloth?' asked Chucky-doddie. They knew all about tablecloths because they had been reared under a hen-coop on the drying green. They had been scolded for leaving dirty foot-marks on a clean tablecloth which was bleaching upon the grass.

The hens slid nervously down the hen ladder on to the snow. No; it was not a tablecloth. Said Tappie-tourie, 'I'll tell you what! I do believe it is the parrot's demerara sugar!' (Now the parrot ought to have told them that demerara sugar is *not* white.) Selina Pickacorn tasted a beakful. 'It is nothing extra special nice; he need not have talked so much about it.' 'How horribly cold and wet it feels.' Just then the farmer came into the field with a horse and cart. He drove the hens back into the hut, fastened the door with a peg, and tied the hut behind his cart with a rope in order to drag it homewards through the snow.

The hen-hut did not run smoothly; it had a tiresome little waggling wheel at one end, that caught in ruts. It bumped along; and the pullets inside it cackled and fluttered. Before the procession had got clear of the field – the hut door flew open. Out bounced Tappie-tourie, Chucky-doddie, Selina Pickacorn, and five other hens. The farmer and his dog caught five of them, none too gently. But the three first-named birds flew back screaming to the spot where the hen-hut had stood originally, before it had been removed.

The farmer was obliged to leave them for the present.

Tappie-tourie, Chucky-doddie, and Selina wandered around in the snow; the field seemed very large and lost under its wide white covering. 'The hut is gone,' said Tappie-tourie, with a brain wave. 'That is so,' agreed Selina Pickacorn, 'we fell out of the hut.' 'What shall we do?' asked Chucky-doddie. 'I see nothing for it but a Christmas picnic,' said Tappie-tourie; 'here is sugar in plenty, but where is the tea and bread and butter?'

Large flakes of snow commenced to fall. 'Perhaps this is the bread and butter coming,' said Tappie-tourie, looking up hopefully at the darkening sky. 'My feather petticoat is getting so wet,' grumbled Chucky-doddie; 'let us try to walk along the top of that wall, towards the wood.' The wall had a thick white topping of snow; it proved to be a most uncomfortable walk, with frequent tumblings off. They crossed Wilfin Beck on a wooden rail. The water below ran dark and sullen between the white banks. By the time they had

reached the wood it was dusk; for the last hundred yards the hens had been floundering through snowdrifts. 'If this is a Christmas picnic – it is horrid! Let us get up into that spruce tree, and roost there till morning.' They managed to fly up. They perched in a  row on the branch, fluffing out their feathers to warm their cold wet feet. They were one speckled hen and two white hens; only the white hens looked quite yellow against the whiter snow. 'The picnic is a long time commencing,' said the speckled hen, Tappie-tourie. It was soon black as pitch amongst the spreading branches of the spruce.

Down below in the glen the waters of the stream tinkled through the ground ice. Now and then there was a soft rushing sound, as the wet snow slipped off the sapling trees that bent beneath its weight, and sprang upwards again, released. Far off in the woods, a branch snapped under its load, like the sound of a gun at night. The stream murmured, flowing darkly. Dead keshes, withered grass, and canes stood up through the snow on its banks, under a fringe of hazel bushes.

Between the stream and the tree where the hens were roosting, there was a white untrodden slope. Only one tree grew there, a very small spruce, a little Christmas tree some four foot high. As the night grew darker – the branches of this little tree became all tipped with light, and wreathed with icicles and chains of frost. Brighter and brighter it shone, until it seemed to bear a hundred fairy lights; not like the yellow gleam of candles, but a clear white incandescent light.

Small voices and music began to mingle with the sound of the water. Up by the snowy banks, from the wood and from the meadow beyond, tripped scores of little shadowy creatures, advancing from the darkness into the light. They trod a circle on the snow around the Christmas tree, dancing gaily hand-in-hand. Rabbits, moles, squirrels, and wood-mice – even the half blind mole, old Samson Velvet, danced hand-in-paw with a woodmouse and a shrew – whilst a hedgehog played the bag-pipes beneath the fairy spruce.

Tappie-tourie and her sisters craned forward on their branch. 'Is the Christmas picnic commencing? May we fly down and share it? Shall we, too, join the dance?' They slid and sidled forward, shaking down a shower of melting snow and ice. 'Cluck, cluck!' cackled the hens, as they clutched and fluttered amongst slippery boughs.

The lights on the Christmas tree quivered, and went out. All was darkness and silence. 'I'm afraid the Christmas picnic was only a dream; we shall have to roost here till morning.' 'Hush! sit still,' said Tappie-tourie, 'it was not us that frightened them away. Something is stirring near the stream! What is it?' The moon shone out between the clouds, throwing long shadows on the snow; shadows of the hazels and tall keshes. A little figure, questing and snuffling, came out into the moonlight: a small brown figure in a buttoned-up long coat. He examined the footsteps on the snow round the Christmas tree. Then, horrible to relate! he came straight up the snowy slope and stood under the spruce; looking up at the hens. He was a disagreeable fusky musky person, called John Stoat Ferret. First he tried to climb the tree, but he could not do so. Then he cried, 'Shoo! shoo!' and threw sticks at the hens. And then he butted against the tree, and tried to shake them down. They clung, cackling and terrified, in the boughs high over head.

Then John Stoat Ferret thought of another plan; he determined to make them dizzy. He set to work. He danced. It was not at all nice dancing. At first he circled slowly; very, very slowly; then gradually faster, faster, faster, until he was spinning like a top. And always a nasty fusky musky smell steamed upwards into the tree. Tappie-tourie, Chucky-doddie, and Selina Pickacorn, overhead, watched him. They had left off clucking; they watched him in fascinated terrified silence, craning over their branch. And still he spun round and round and round, and the fusky smell rose up into the spruce. Tappie-tourie twisted her head round, following his movements as he danced. And Chucky-doddie twisted her neck round. And Selina Pickacorn not only twisted her head, she began to turn herself upon the branch. All the hens were growing giddy.

John Stoat Ferret danced and spun more furiously, the fusky musky smell rose higher. All three hens commenced to turn round dizzily. In another minute they would fall off. John Stoat Ferret capered and twirled. But all of a sudden he stopped. He sat up, motionless, listening. Voices were approaching up in the cart road that skirts the wood.

Upon Christmas Eve it is a pleasant custom amongst the Big Folk for carol singers to go singing from farm to farm; even to the lonely cottages on the outskirts of the great woods.

Two small boys, who had been out with the carollers, were going home to supper. Their Christmas picnic had been more prosperous than poor Tappie-tourie's. Their pockets were full of apples and toffy and pennies.

'George,' said Jimmy, 'give us a ginger snap.'

'Na-a!' said George, 'it will gummy your teeth tegidder, that you cannot sing. Whooop!' shouted George, jumping into a snowdrift, 'sing another –

> "Wassail, wassail! to our town!
> The bowl is white, and the ale is brown;
> The bowl is made of the rosemary tree, and so is the ale,
>   of the good barlee.
> Little maid, little maid, tirl the pin!
> Open the door, and let us come in!"

John Stoat Ferret listened intently. 'Whooop!' shouted Jimmy, kicking the snow about, and swinging his candle lantern; 'sing another one –

> "Here us comes a wassailing, under the holly green,
> Here us comes a wandering, so merry to be seen.
> Good luck good Master Hodgin, and kind Mistress also,
> And all the little childer that round the table go!
> Your pockets full of money, your cupboards of good
>   Cheer,
> A merry Christmas, Guizzards, and a Happy New
>   Year!"

'Jimmy!' exclaimed George suddenly, 'I smell stoat. Look over the wall with the lantern.' John Stoat Ferret departed hurriedly. And as if a spell were broken, Chucky-doddie, Tappie-tourie, and Selina found their voices. They cackled loudly, up in the tree. 'Eh, sithee!' said George, 'them's our three hens that father lost out of t' hen-hut. Fetch 'em down: I'se haud lantern.' 'This wall's gaily slape!' giggled Jimmy, balancing himself on the slippery top stones. He reached up into the tree, and got hold of Tappie-tourie first, by the legs. 'Ketch!' said he, and flung her into the snowdrift in the lane. 'Here's another fat 'un!' He threw Chucky-doddie across. Selina flew after them of her own accord. The boys picked the hens out of the snow, and trudged homewards; George, with a hen tucked under each arm; and Jimmy, with one hen and the candle lantern. It was an inglorious ending to Tappie-tourie's Christmas picnic; but at one time it looked like ending much worse.

The End

Christmas Festivities

Christmas celebrations are a highlight of any rabbit's festive calendar, as Beatrix Potter described in this letter, written on behalf of Peter Rabbit and his cousin, Benjamin Bunny.

Today Benjamin Bunny and I have been choosing our Christmas tree. We went to a wood where there are nut bushes and cherry trees and oak coppice; and in a cleared space amongst the oaks we found a plantation of young fir trees. We chose a lovely little tree 4 feet high. Said Benjamin, standing on his hind legs – "I'm afraid it is too big, Peter; we could not reach the top to tie on apples and nuts and fairy candles." But I said – "It is just right Benjamin; Twinkleberry will climb up and help us; not Nutkin, he would crack the nuts."

You know we do not move our tree; we leave it growing in the wood. When Christmas-tide is over, it looks like any other little fir tree. But you should see it on Christmas Eve! All aglow with fairy lights, and hung with hips and haws and holly berries, & nutcrackers and mouse toffee in silver paper, and nutcrackers, and garlanded with chains of sparkling icicles. Then all of us little animals dance round, around, around, while Cock Robin sings overhead and Pricklepin plays the bagpipes. And we shout and sing so loud that you may hear us through the dark, wishing you all a Merry Christmas and a Happy New Year!

Yours affectionately,

Peter Rabbit

And here is the beautiful tree in all its glory!
Which other characters can you spot dancing in the ring?

Beatrix Potter

THE TAILOR OF
GLOUCESTER

"I'LL BE AT CHARGES FOR A LOOKING-GLASS;
AND ENTERTAIN A SCORE OR TWO OF TAILORS."
Richard III

ABOUT THIS BOOK

The Tailor of Gloucester was Beatrix Potter's own favourite among all
her books. She first heard the true story on which it is based when
visiting her cousin, Caroline Hutton, who lived near Gloucester.
Leaving an unfinished waistcoat for the Mayor of Gloucester in his
shop one Saturday morning, a tailor was amazed to find it ready on
the Monday, except for one buttonhole, for which there was "no more
twist". In reality, his two assistants had secretly completed the job, but
Beatrix Potter has the work finished by little brown mice. She adds an
extra note of enchantment by setting the story on one of the most
magical nights of the year, Christmas Eve, when animals can talk, and
weaving in many of her favourite traditional rhymes.

IN THE TIME of swords and periwigs and full-skirted coats with flowered lappets when gentlemen wore ruffles, and gold-laced waistcoats of paduasoy and taffeta — there lived a tailor in Gloucester.

He sat in the window of a little shop in Westgate Street, cross-legged on a table, from morning till dark.

All day long while the light lasted he sewed and snippeted, piecing out his satin and pompadour, and lute-string; stuffs had strange names, and were very expensive in the days of the Tailor of Gloucester.

But although he sewed fine silk for his neighbours, he himself was very, very poor — a little old man in spectacles, with a pinched face, old crooked fingers, and a suit of thread-bare clothes.

He cut his coats without waste, according to his embroidered cloth; they were very small ends and snippets that lay about upon the table — "Too narrow breadths for nought — except waistcoats for mice," said the tailor.

One bitter cold day near Christmas-time the tailor began to make a coat — a coat of cherry-coloured corded silk embroidered with pansies and roses, and a cream-coloured satin waist-coat — trimmed with gauze and green worsted chenille — for the Mayor of Gloucester.

The tailor worked and worked, and he talked to himself. He measured the silk, and turned it round and round, and trimmed it into shape with his shears; the table was all littered with cherry-coloured snippets.

"No breadth at all, and cut on the cross; it is no breadth at all; tippets for mice and ribbons for mobs! for mice!" said the Tailor of Gloucester.

When the snow-flakes came down against the small leaded window-panes and shut out the light, the tailor had done his day's work; all the silk and satin lay cut out upon the table.

There were twelve pieces for the coat and four pieces for the waistcoat; and there were pocket flaps and cuffs, and buttons all in

order. For the lining of the coat there was fine yellow taffeta; and for the button-holes of the waist-coat, there was cherry-coloured twist. And everything was ready to sew together in the morning, all measured and sufficient — except that there was wanting just one single skein of cherry-coloured twisted silk.

The tailor came out of his shop at dark, for he did not sleep there at nights; he fastened the window and locked the door, and took away the

key. No one lived there at night but little brown mice, and they run in and out without any keys!

For behind the wooden wainscots of all the old houses in Gloucester, there are little mouse staircases and secret trap-doors; and the mice run from house to house through those long narrow passages; they can run all over the town without going into the streets.

But the tailor came out of his shop, and shuffled home through the snow. He lived quite near by in College Court, next the doorway to College Green; and although it was not a big house, the tailor was so poor he only rented the kitchen.

He lived alone with his cat; it was called Simpkin.

Now all day long while the tailor was out at work, Simpkin kept house by himself; and he also was fond of the mice, though he gave them no satin for coats!

"Miaw?" said the cat when the tailor opened the door, "miaw?"

The tailor replied — "Simpkin, we shall make our fortune, but I am worn to a ravelling. Take this groat (which is our last fourpence) and Simpkin, take a china pipkin; buy a penn'orth of bread, a penn'orth of milk and a penn'orth of sausages.

And oh, Simpkin, with the last penny of our fourpence buy me one penn'orth of cherry-coloured silk. But do not lose the last penny of the fourpence, Simpkin, or I am undone and worn to a thread-paper, for I have NO MORE TWIST."

Then Simpkin again said "Miaw?" and took the groat and the pipkin, and went out into the dark.

The tailor was very tired and beginning to be ill. He sat down by the hearth and talked to himself about that wonderful coat.

"I shall make my fortune — to be cut bias — the Mayor of Gloucester is to be married on Christmas Day in the morning, and he hath ordered a coat and an embroidered waistcoat — to be lined with yellow taffeta — and the taffeta sufficeth; there is no more left over in snippets than will serve to make tippets for mice —"

Then the tailor started; for suddenly, interrupting him, from the dresser at the other side of the kitchen came a number of little noises —

Tip tap, tip tap, tip tap tip!

"Now what can that be?" said the Tailor of Gloucester, jumping up from his chair. The dresser was covered with crockery and pipkins, willow pattern plates, and tea-cups and mugs.

The tailor crossed the kitchen, and stood quite still beside the dresser, listening, and peering through his spectacles. Again from under a tea-cup, came those funny little noises —

Tip tap, tip tap, tip tap tip!

"This is very peculiar," said the Tailor of Gloucester; and he lifted up the tea-cup which was upside down.

Out stepped a little live lady mouse, and made a curtsey to the tailor! Then she hopped away down off the dresser, and under the wainscot.

The tailor sat down again by the fire, warming his poor cold hands, and mumbling to himself —

"The waistcoat is cut out from peach-coloured satin — tambour stitch and rose-buds in beautiful floss silk! Was I wise to entrust my last fourpence to Simpkin? One-and-twenty button-holes of cherry-coloured twist!"

But all at once, from the dresser, there came other little noises —

Tip tap, tip tap, tip tap tip!

"This is passing extraordinary!" said the Tailor of Gloucester, and turned over another tea-cup, which was up-side down.

Out stepped a little gentleman mouse, and made a bow to the tailor!

And then from all over the dresser came a chorus of little tappings, all sounding together, and answering one another, like watch-beetles in an old worm-eaten window-shutter —

Tip tap, tip tap, tip tap tip!

And out from under tea-cups and from under bowls and basins, stepped other and more little mice, who hopped away down off the dresser and under the wainscot.

The tailor sat down, close over the fire, lamenting — "One-and-twenty button-holes of cherry-coloured silk! To be finished by noon of Saturday; and this is Tuesday evening. Was it right to let loose those mice, undoubtedly the property of Simpkin? Alack, I am undone, for I have no more twist!"

The little mice came out again, and listened to the tailor; they took notice of the pattern of that wonderful coat. They whispered to one another about the taffeta lining, and about little mouse tippets.

And then all at once they all ran away together down the passage behind the wainscot, squeaking and calling to one another, as they ran from house to house; and not one mouse was left in the tailor's kitchen when Simpkin came back with the pipkin of milk!

Simpkin opened the door and bounced in, with an angry "G-r-r-miaw!" like a cat that is vexed; for he hated the snow, and there was snow in his ears, and snow in his collar at the back of his neck. He put down the loaf and the sausages upon the dresser, and sniffed.

"Simpkin," said the tailor, "where is my twist?"

But Simpkin set down the pipkin of milk upon the dresser, and looked suspiciously at the tea-cups. He wanted his supper of little fat mouse!

"Simpkin," said the tailor, "where is my TWIST?"

But Simpkin hid a little parcel privately in the tea-pot, and spit and growled at the tailor; and if Simpkin had been able to talk, he would have asked — "Where is my MOUSE?"

"Alack, I am undone!" said the Tailor of Gloucester, and went sadly to bed.

All that night long Simpkin hunted and searched through the kitchen, peeping into cupboards and under the wainscot, and into the tea-pot where he had hidden that twist; but still he found never a mouse!

Whenever the tailor muttered and talked in his sleep, Simpkin said "Miaw-ger-r-w-s-s-ch!" and made strange horrid noises, as cats do at night.

For the poor old tailor was very ill with a fever, tossing and turning in his four-post bed; and still in his dreams he mumbled — "No more twist! no more twist!"

All that day he was ill, and the next day, and the next; and what should become of the cherry-coloured coat? In the tailor's shop in Westgate Street the embroidered silk and satin lay cut out upon the table — one-and-twenty button-holes — and who should come to sew them, when the window was barred, and the door was fast locked?

But that does not hinder the little brown mice; they run in and out without any keys through all the old houses in Gloucester!

Out of doors the market folks went trudging through the snow to buy their geese and turkeys, and to bake their Christmas pies; but there would be no Christmas dinner for Simpkin and the poor old Tailor of Gloucester.

The tailor lay ill for three days and nights; and then it was Christmas Eve, and very late at night. The moon climbed up over the roofs and chimneys, and looked down over the gateway into College Court. There were no lights in the windows, nor any sound in the houses; all the city of Gloucester was fast asleep under the snow.

And still Simpkin wanted his mice, and he mewed as he stood beside the four-post bed.

But it is in the old story that all the beasts can talk, in the night between Christmas Eve and Christmas Day in the morning (though there are very few folk that can hear them, or know what it is that they say).

When the Cathedral clock struck twelve there was an answer — like an echo of the chimes — and Simpkin heard it, and came out of the tailor's door, and wandered about in the snow.

From all the roofs and gables and old wooden houses in Gloucester came a thousand merry voices singing the old Christmas rhymes — all the old songs that ever I heard of, and some that I don't know, like Whittington's bells.

First and loudest the cocks cried out — "Dame, get up, and bake your pies!"

"Oh, dilly, dilly, dilly!" sighed Simpkin.

And now in a garret there were lights and sounds of dancing, and cats came from over the way.

"Hey, diddle, diddle, the cat and the fiddle! All the cats in Gloucester — except me," said Simpkin.

Under the wooden eaves the starlings and sparrows sang of Christmas pies; the jack-daws woke up in the Cathedral tower; and although it was the middle of the night the throstles and robins sang; the air was quite full of little twittering tunes.

But it was all rather provoking to poor hungry Simpkin!

Particularly he was vexed with some little shrill voices from behind a wooden lattice. I think that they were bats, because they always have

very small voices — especially in a black frost, when they talk in their sleep, like the Tailor of Gloucester.

They said something mysterious that sounded like —

"Buz, quoth the blue fly; hum, quoth
    the bee;
  Buz and hum they cry, and so do we!"

and Simpkin went away shaking his ears as if he had a bee in his bonnet.

From the tailor's shop in Westgate came a glow of light; and when Simpkin crept up to peep in at the window it was full of candles. There was a snippeting of scissors, and snappeting of thread; and little mouse voices sang loudly and gaily —

"Four-and-twenty tailors
  Went to catch a snail,
  The best man amongst them
  Durst not touch her tail;
  She put out her horns
  Like a little kyloe cow,
  Run, tailors, run! or she'll
    have you all e'en now!"

Then without a pause the little mouse voices went on again —

"Sieve my lady's oatmeal,
  Grind my lady's flour,
  Put it in a chestnut,
  Let it stand an hour —"

"Mew! Mew!" interrupted Simpkin, and he scratched at the door.

But the key was under the tailor's pillow; he could not get in.
The little mice only laughed, and tried another tune —

"Three little mice sat down to spin,
  Pussy passed by and she peeped in.
What are you at, my fine little men?
Making coats for gentlemen.
Shall I come in and cut off your
    threads?
Oh, no, Miss Pussy, you'd bite off
    our heads!"

"Mew! Mew!" cried Simpkin.
"Hey diddle dinketty?" answered the little mice —

"Hey diddle dinketty, poppetty pet!
  The merchants of London they
    wear scarlet;
  Silk in the collar, and gold in the
    hem,
  So merrily march the merchantmen!"

They clicked their thimbles to mark the time, but none of the songs pleased Simpkin; he sniffed and mewed at the door of the shop.

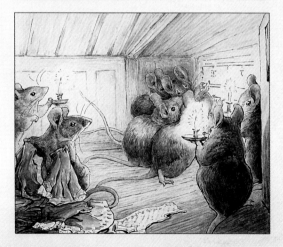

"And then I bought
  A pipkin and a popkin,
  A slipkin and a slopkin,
  All for one farthing —

and upon the kitchen dresser!" added the rude little mice.

"Mew! scratch! scratch!" scuffled Simpkin on the window-sill; while the little mice inside sprang to their feet, and all began to shout at once in little twittering voices — "No more twist! No more twist!" And they barred up the window shutters and shut out Simpkin.

But still through the nicks in the shutters he could hear the click of thimbles, and little mouse voices singing —

"No more twist! No more twist!"

Simpkin came away from the shop and went home, considering in his mind. He found the poor old tailor without fever, sleeping peacefully.

Then Simpkin went on tip-toe and took a little parcel of silk out of the tea-pot, and looked at it in the moonlight; and he felt quite ashamed of his badness compared with those good little mice!

When the tailor awoke in the morning, the first thing which he saw, upon the patchwork quilt, was a skein of cherry-coloured twisted silk, and beside his bed stood the repentant Simpkin!

"Alack, I am worn to a ravelling," said the Tailor of Gloucester, "but I have my twist!"

The sun was shining on the snow when the tailor got up and dressed, and came out into the street with Simpkin running before him.

The starlings whistled on the chimney stacks, and the throstles and robins sang — but they sang their own little noises, not the words they had sung in the night.

"Alack," said the tailor, "I have my twist; but no more strength — nor time — than will serve to make me one single button-hole; for this

is Christmas Day in the Morning!
The Mayor of Gloucester shall
be married by noon — and where is
his cherry-coloured coat?"

He unlocked the door of the
little shop in Westgate Street,
and Simpkin ran in, like a cat that
expects something.

But there was no one there!
Not even one little brown mouse!

The boards were swept and
clean; the little ends of thread
and the little silk snippets were
all tidied away, and gone from off
the floor.

But upon the table — oh joy! the tailor gave a shout — there, where
he had left plain cuttings of silk — there lay the most beautifullest
coat and embroidered satin waistcoat that ever were worn by a Mayor
of Gloucester!

There were roses and pansies
upon the facings of the coat; and
the waistcoat was worked with
poppies and corn-flowers.

Everything was finished except
just one single cherry-coloured
button-hole, and where that
button-hole was wanting there
was pinned a scrap of paper with
these words — in little teeny
weeny writing —

NO MORE TWIST

And from then began the luck of the Tailor of Gloucester; he grew quite stout, and he grew quite rich.

He made the most wonderful waistcoats for all the rich merchants of Gloucester, and for all the fine gentlemen of the country round.

Never were seen such ruffles, or such embroidered cuffs and lappets! But his button-holes were the greatest triumph of it all.

The stitches of those button-holes were so neat — *so* neat — I wonder how they could be stitched by an old man in spectacles, with crooked old fingers, and a tailor's thimble.

The stitches of those button-holes were so small — *so* small — they looked as if they had been made by little mice!

The End

'I SAW THREE SHIPS'

Beatrix Potter's first edition of *The Tailor of Gloucester*, published privately
before the Warne edition of 1903, included this popular Christmas ditty.

I SAW THREE SHIPS come sailing by,
  Sailing by, sailing by;
I saw three ships come sailing by,
  On Christmas Day in the morning.

And who do you think were in them then,
  In them then, in them then?
And who do you think were in them then,
  On Christmas Day in the morning?

Three pretty maids were in them then,
  In them then, in them then;
Three pretty maids were in them then,
  On Christmas Day in the morning.

And one could whistle, and one could sing,
  And one could play on the violin;
Such joy was at my wedding,
  On Christmas Day in the morning!

Christmas Mischief

Christmas is a time for feasting with your friends but, as these letters written by Beatrix Potter show, not everyone is on their best behaviour during the festive season.

Miss Jenny Wren,
The Nest,
Beech Hedge.

Dear Miss Jenny,
Will you accept a little cask
of currant wine from your trusted
friend Cock Robin! The carrier
will leave it at the garden gate.

Cock Robin

Cock Robin Esq.,
The Holly Bush.

Dear Cock Robin,
I thank you kindly for the
little cask of currant wine.
I have worked a new little
scarlet waistcoat for you.
Will you dine with me
on Christmas Day on the
parlour window sill?

Yr. aff. friend,
Jenny Wren

Jack Sparrow,
The Eaves.

Dear Jack Sparrow,
I have overheard that Jenny Wren
& Cock Robin are going to eat
their Christmas dinner on the
parlour window sill. Let's all go
and gobble up the crumbs. Bring
Dick Chaffinch and I'll tell the
starlings.
Yr. friend in mischief,
Tom Titmouse

THE TALE OF
BENJAMIN BUNNY

ABOUT THIS BOOK

The real-life Benjamin Bunny was a tame rabbit of Beatrix Potter's, whom she sketched constantly, and whose exploits continually amused her. "He is an abject coward, but believes in bluster, could stare our old dog out of countenance, chase a cat that has turned tail." Although Benjamin had died by 1904, when this story was published, Beatrix may well have been thinking of him when she created Peter Rabbit's cousin. Little Benjamin Bunny is a very self-possessed animal, who makes himself quite at home in Mr. McGregor's garden.

While Peter and Benjamin do get into all sorts of trouble, they are not always mischievous. Beatrix painted plenty of Christmas cards and illustrations which show the cousins being incredibly helpful, delivering cards and parcels.

ONE MORNING a little rabbit sat on a bank. He pricked his ears and listened to the trit-trot, trit-trot of a pony.

A gig was coming along the road; it was driven by Mr. McGregor, and beside him sat Mrs. McGregor in her best bonnet.

As soon as they had passed, little Benjamin Bunny slid down into the road, and set off — with a hop, skip and a jump — to call upon his relations, who lived in the wood at the back of Mr. McGregor's garden.

That wood was full of rabbit-holes; and in the neatest sandiest hole of all, lived Benjamin's aunt and his cousins — Flopsy, Mopsy, Cotton-tail and Peter.

Old Mrs. Rabbit was a widow; she earned her living by knitting rabbit-wool mittens and muffetees (I once bought a pair at a bazaar). She also sold herbs, and rosemary tea, and rabbit-tobacco (which is what *we* call lavender).

Little Benjamin did not very much want to see his Aunt.

He came round the back of the fir-tree, and nearly tumbled upon the top of his Cousin Peter.

Peter was sitting by himself. He looked poorly, and was dressed in a red cotton pocket-handkerchief.

"Peter," — said little Benjamin, in a whisper — "who has got
your clothes?"

Peter replied — "The scarecrow in Mr. McGregor's garden," and described how he had been chased about the garden, and had dropped his shoes and coat.

Little Benjamin sat down beside his cousin, and assured him that Mr. McGregor had gone out in a gig, and Mrs. McGregor also; and certainly for the day, because she was wearing her best bonnet.

Peter said he hoped that it would rain.

At this point, old Mrs. Rabbit's voice was heard inside the rabbit-hole, calling — "Cotton-tail! Cotton-tail! fetch some more camomile!"

Peter said he thought he might feel better if he went for a walk.

They went away hand in
hand, and got upon the
flat top of the wall at
the bottom of the wood.
From here they looked
down into Mr. McGregor's
garden. Peter's coat and
shoes were plainly to be
seen upon the scarecrow,
topped with an old
tam-o-shanter of
Mr. McGregor's.

Little Benjamin said,
"It spoils people's clothes
to squeeze under a gate;
the proper way to get in, is
to climb down a pear tree."

Peter fell down head
first; but it was of no
consequence, as the bed
below was newly raked
and quite soft.

It had been sown with
lettuces.

They left a great many odd little foot-marks all over the bed, especially little Benjamin, who was wearing clogs.

Little Benjamin said that the first thing to be done was to get back Peter's clothes, in order that they might be able to use the pocket-handkerchief.

They took them off the scarecrow. There had been rain during the night; there was water in the shoes, and the coat was somewhat shrunk.

Benjamin tried on the tam-o-shanter, but it was too big for him.

Then he suggested that they should fill the pocket-handkerchief with onions, as a little present for his Aunt.

Peter did not seem to be enjoying himself; he kept hearing noises.

Benjamin, on the contrary, was perfectly at home, and ate a lettuce leaf. He said that he was in the habit of coming to the garden with his father to get lettuces for their Sunday dinner.

(The name of little Benjamin's papa was old Mr. Benjamin Bunny.)

The lettuces certainly were very fine.

Peter did not eat anything; he said he should like to go home. Presently he dropped half the onions.

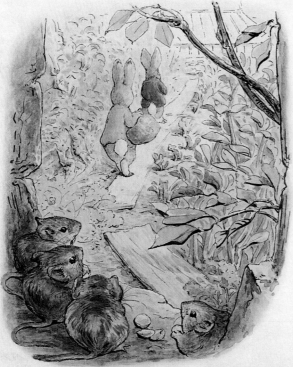

Little Benjamin said that it was not possible to get back up the pear tree, with a load of vegetables. He led the way boldly towards the other end of the garden. They went along a little walk on planks, under a sunny red-brick wall.

The mice sat on their door-steps cracking cherry-stones; they winked at Peter Rabbit and little Benjamin Bunny.

Presently Peter let the pocket-handkerchief go again.

They got amongst flower-pots, and frames and tubs; Peter heard noises worse than ever, his eyes were as big as lolly-pops!

He was a step or two in front of his cousin, when he suddenly stopped.

This is what those little rabbits saw round that corner!

Little Benjamin took one look, and then, in half a minute less than no time, he hid himself and Peter and the onions underneath a large basket . . .

The cat got up and stretched herself, and came and sniffed at the basket.

Perhaps she liked the smell of onions!

Anyway, she sat down upon the top of the basket.

She sat there for *five hours*.

*

I cannot draw you a picture
of Peter and Benjamin
underneath the basket,
because it was quite dark,
and because the smell of
onions was fearful; it made
Peter Rabbit and little
Benjamin cry.

The sun got round behind the wood, and it was quite late in the
afternoon; but still the cat sat upon the basket.

At length there was a
pitter-patter, pitter-patter,
and some bits of mortar
fell from the wall above.

   The cat looked up and
saw old Mr. Benjamin
Bunny prancing along
the top of the wall of the
upper terrace.

   He was smoking a pipe
of rabbit-tobacco, and had
a little switch in his hand.

   He was looking for his son.

Old Mr. Bunny had no opinion whatever of cats.

He took a tremendous jump off the top of the wall on to the top of the cat, and cuffed it off the basket, and kicked it into the green-house, scratching off a handful of fur.

The cat was too much surprised to scratch back.

When old Mr. Bunny had driven the cat into the green-house, he locked the door.

Then he came back to the basket and took out his son Benjamin by the ears, and whipped him with the little switch.

Then he took out his nephew Peter.

Then he took out the handkerchief of onions, and marched out of the garden.

When Mr. McGregor returned about half an hour later, he observed several things which perplexed him.

It looked as though some person had been walking all over the garden in a pair of clogs — only the foot-marks were too ridiculously little!

Also he could not understand how the cat could have managed to shut herself up *inside* the green-house, locking the door upon the *outside*.

When Peter got home, his mother forgave him, because she was so glad to see that he had found his shoes and coat. Cotton-tail and Peter folded up the pocket-handkerchief, and old Mrs. Rabbit strung up the onions and hung them from the kitchen ceiling, with the bunches of herbs and the rabbit-tobacco.

The End

WAG~BY~WALL

'Footprints in the Snow' by Beatrix Potter (5th March 1909)

ABOUT THIS BOOK

The story that was to become *Wag-by-Wall* was begun by Beatrix Potter in 1909, and was at that time called *The Little Black Kettle*. It was not published until 1944, the year after Beatrix Potter's death, when it appeared in an anniversary edition of *The Horn Book Magazine*. The tale has a fairy-tale quality about it, and tells the story of an old woman who is reunited with her grand-daughter. Beatrix always thought of it as an accompaniment to *The Tailor of Gloucester*, as one tells the story of a lonely old man, the other of a lonely old woman, and both are tinged with Christmas magic.

Beatrix Potter never illustrated this tale herself, so we have selected some of her lesser-known watercolours to accompany the story.

ONCE UPON A TIME there was an old woman called Sally Benson who lived alone in a little thatched cottage. She had a garden and two fields, and there was grazing for a cow on the bog in summer while the fields were shut off to grow hay grass.

While her husband was alive, and able to work, they had lived comfortably. He worked for a farmer, while Sally milked the cow and fed their pig at home. After Sally became a widow she had a hard struggle. Tom Benson's long illness had left debts.

The cottage had belonged to Sally's mother, and to her grandparents before her. Her grandfather had been a cattle dealer. He bought and sold cattle at fairs, and made a bit of money. Nobody knew what he had done with it. He did not seem to spend much; and he never gave away one farthing. The old furniture was poor and plain; the only handsome piece that had belonged to the old man was 'Wag-by-the-wall' the clock. 'Tic tock: gold toes: tic: tock: gold: toes,' it repeated over and over; till any body might have felt provoked to throw a shoe at it – 'Tic: tock: gold: toes:'

Sally took no notice. The clock had been saying those words ever since she was born. Nobody knew what it meant. Sally thought the world of the clock; and she loved her old singing kettle. She boiled water in it to make balm tea. She made it in a jug, and she grew the lemon-scented balm in her own garden. The kettle had been cracked and mended more than once.

The last time Sally took it to the smithy, Isaac Blacksmith

looked at it over his spectacles and said – 'More patch than bottom. It will cost you more than a new kettle.' 'Nay, nay! thou mun patch it, Isaac Blacksmith! I tell thee, thou mun patch it, and thou mun patch it again!' Sally stood on tiptoes to whisper – 'I tell thee – it can sing.' 'Aye, aye? like a toom barrel?' said Isaac Blacksmith, blowing the bellows.

So Sally went on using her old kettle, and it sang to her. The kettle sang on the hearth, and the bees sang in the garden, where she grew old-fashioned flowers as well as potatoes and cabbages. There were wall flowers, pansies and roses in their season; balm for her own herb tea; and thyme, hyssop and borage that the honey bees love.

When Sally sat knitting by the cottage door she listened to the bees – 'Arise – work – pray: Night follows day: Sweet Summer's day.' The bees hummed drowsily amongst the flowers – 'To bed with sun: day's work well done.' The bees went home into their hives at dusk.

Presently, indoors, the kettle began to sing; at first it sang gently and slowly, then faster and faster and more loud, as it came to boiling and bubbling over. It sang words something like this – to the tune of Ash grove –

'With pomp power and glory the world beckons vainly,
    In chase of such vanities why should I roam?
While peace and content bless my little thatched cottage,
    And warm my own hearth with the treasures of home.'

Sally Benson sitting by her fire on a winter's evening listened to the song of the kettle and she was contented. The cottage was warm and dry; it was whitewashed within and without, and spotlessly clean. There was no upstairs; only the kitchen, with cupboards and a box bed in the wall; and behind the kitchen was another tiny room and a pantry. Sally thought it was a palace; she had no wish to live in a big house.

Above the kitchen hearth at the south end of the cottage, there was a tall stone chimney stack standing up above the roof. Dry thatch is dangerous for catching fire from sparks, but there was plenty of green moss and house leek growing beside Sally Benson's chimney. Under the same long low roof at the north end was a wood shed.

A pair of white owls lived in the shed. Every summer, year after year, they nested there – though it could scarcely be called a 'nest'. The hen owl just laid four eggs on a bare board under the rafters. The little owlets were like balls of fluff, with big dark eyes. The youngest owlet, that hatched out of the last laid egg, was always smaller than the other three. Sally called him Benjamin.

When the little owlets were old enough to come out, they climbed up the thatch and sat in a row on the ridge of the roof. They hissed and craned their necks, and twisted their heads to watch their parents, mousing over the bog. The old owls flitted noiselessly over the coarse grass and rushes; they looked like great white moths in the twilight.

As the young owlets grew older, they became more and more hungry – the mother owl used to come out hunting food by daylight in the afternoons. The peewits over the bog swooped at her, crying and wailing, although she only sought for mice. Little breezes stirred the cotton grass; and Nancy Cow, knee deep in sedge and meadow sweet, blew warm breath lazily. Her big feet squelched amongst moss and eyebright and sundew; she turned back to firm turf and lay down to wait until Sally's voice called her home for milking.

When the old owls brought back mice they fed each wide gaping mouth in turn. Amongst the jostling and hissing and snatching, Benjamin was often knocked over. Sometimes he rolled down the thatch and fell off the roof. Sally picked him up and put him back. If the night had been wet she dried him by the fire. One morning she found all four baby owlets on the door step hissing at the cat.

Sally was very fond of the owls. Indeed she was fond of all things; a smiling friendly old woman with cheeks like withered apples.

But 'good times and hard times – all times go over'. While the hard times lasted they hit poor Sally very hard. There came a year of famine. Rain spoilt the hay and harvest, blight ruined the potato crop. Sally's pig died, and she was forced to sell her cow to pay the debts. There seemed to be nothing for it but to sell the cottage also, and end her days in the Poor House. She had nobody that she could turn to, no one to ask for help.

She and Tom had lost their only child – a daughter. Such a dear pretty girl she had been, with yellow curls, rosy cheeks, and blue eyes always laughing, until she ran away to marry a wastrel. Sally had sent money when a baby girl was born – another little 'Goldie-locks'. Time and again they wrote for money. When Sally had no more to send them they faded out of sight.

On Christmas Eve Sally Benson sat by the fire reading a letter, which the postman had brought her. It was a sad letter, written by a stranger. It said that her daughter and her son-in-law were dead, and that a neighbour – the writer – had taken in their child into her home out of pity. 'A bonny child she is; a right little Goldie-locks; eight years old, and tidy and helpful. She will be a comfort to her Grannie. Please send money to pay her fare, and I will set her on her way. I have five mouths to feed so I cannot keep her long. Please send money soon, Mrs. Benson.' Poor Sally! with no money and no prospect but the Poor House.

That Christmas Eve in the moonlight, a white owl sat on the chimney stack. When a cloud came over the moon, the owl dozed. Perhaps a wisp of blue smoke floating upwards made him sleepy – He swayed forward and fell into the chimney.

Down below Sally Benson sat by the hearth, watching the dying fire. One hand crumpled the letter in the pocket of her old black skirt; the other thin trembling hand was twisted in her apron. Tears ran down her poor old nose; she mopped them with her apron. She was crying for little Goldie-locks. She sat on and on, into the night.

At length there was a noise high up in the chimney. There came a rush of soot and stones; small stones and mortar came first. Several large heavy stones tumbled after; and the white owl on the top.

'Save us! what a dirty mess!' said Sally, scrambling to her feet and forgetting her troubles. She picked up the owl gently, and blew the soot off him, and set him on a chair. The soft feather tip of one wing was scorched; otherwise he was unhurt. But the soot had got into his eyes and his gullet; he blinked and gasped and choked. Sally fetched a drop of milk and fed him with a spoon.

Then she turned to sweep up the mess on the hearth. There was a smell of charred wood and burning wool. Amongst the stones was a black thing which smoked. It was an old stocking tied round the ankle with a bit of string. The foot was full of something heavy. Gold showed through a hole in the toes. 'Tic: toc: gold: toes:' said Wag-by-the-wall the clock.

Something seemed to have happened to Wag-by-the-wall; he went whirr, whirra, whirr! trying to strike. When he struck at last he struck 14 instead of 12; and he changed his tick. Instead of saying 'Tic: toc: gold: toes: tic: toc: gold: toes!' he said 'Tick:er: tocks: Goldie: locks: tick:er: tocks: Goldie: locks,' and those were his words ever after.

Sally Benson fetched her little grand-daughter to live with her. She bought another cow, and a pig, and she grew potatoes and balm and sweet flowers in her garden for the honey bees. And every summer the white owls nested in the wood shed.

Sally enjoyed a cheerful contented old age, and little Goldie-locks grew up and married a young farmer. They lived happily ever after, and they always kept the singing kettle and Wag-by-Wall the clock.

The End

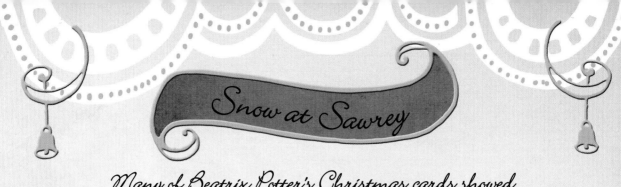

Snow at Sawrey

Many of Beatrix Potter's Christmas cards showed
scenes of her rabbit characters playing in the snow.

THE TALE OF
THE FLOPSY BUNNIES

ABOUT THIS BOOK

The Tale of The Flopsy Bunnies pays another visit to the world of Peter Rabbit and Benjamin Bunny. Both rabbits have now grown up, Benjamin has married Peter's sister Flopsy and, although still "improvident and cheerful", has a large family to care for. Beatrix Potter was well aware that her earlier books had created a huge demand for rabbit stories, and dedicated this one, "For all little friends of Mr. McGregor and Peter and Benjamin". Besides, she enjoyed painting rabbits, and gardens too. The tale introduces Mrs. Thomasina Tittlemouse, who later got a whole story to herself in *The Tale of Mrs. Tittlemouse*, and who, in this story, receives a generous Christmas present from the Flopsy Bunnies.

IT IS SAID that the effect of eating too much lettuce is "soporific".

I have never felt sleepy after eating lettuces; but then *I* am not a rabbit.

They certainly had a very soporific effect upon the Flopsy Bunnies!

When Benjamin Bunny grew up, he married his Cousin Flopsy. They had a large family, and they were very improvident and cheerful.

I do not remember the separate names of their children; they were generally called the "Flopsy Bunnies".

As there was not always quite enough to eat — Benjamin used to borrow cabbages from Flopsy's brother, Peter Rabbit, who kept a nursery garden.

Sometimes Peter Rabbit had no cabbages to spare.

When this happened, the Flopsy Bunnies went across the field to a rubbish heap, in the ditch outside Mr. McGregor's garden.

Mr. McGregor's rubbish heap was a mixture. There were jam pots and paper bags, and mountains of chopped grass from the mowing machine (which always tasted oily), and some rotten vegetable marrows and an old boot or two. One day — oh joy! — there were a quantity of overgrown lettuces, which had "shot" into flower.

The Flopsy Bunnies simply
stuffed lettuces. By degrees,
one after another, they were
overcome with slumber, and lay
down in the mown grass.

Benjamin was not so much
overcome as his children. Before
going to sleep he was sufficiently
wide awake to put a paper bag
over his head to keep off the flies.

The little Flopsy Bunnies slept
delightfully in the warm sun.
From the lawn beyond the
garden came the distant
clacketty sound of the mowing
machine. The bluebottles
buzzed about the wall, and a
little old mouse picked over the
rubbish among the jam pots.

(I can tell you her name, she was
called Thomasina Tittlemouse, a
wood-mouse with a long tail.)

She rustled across the paper bag,
and awakened Benjamin Bunny.

The mouse apologized profusely,
and said that she knew Peter Rabbit.

While she and Benjamin were talking, close under the wall, they heard a heavy tread above their heads; and suddenly Mr. McGregor emptied out a sackful of lawn mowings right upon the top of the sleeping Flopsy Bunnies! Benjamin shrank down under his paper bag. The mouse hid in a jam pot.

The little rabbits smiled sweetly in their sleep under the shower of grass; they did not awake because the lettuces had been so soporific.

They dreamt that their mother Flopsy was tucking them up in a hay bed.

Mr. McGregor looked down after emptying his sack. He saw some funny little brown tips of ears sticking up through the lawn mowings. He stared at them for some time.

Presently a fly settled on one of them and it moved.

Mr. McGregor climbed down on to the rubbish heap —

"One, two, three, four! five! six leetle rabbits!" said he as he dropped them into his sack.

The Flopsy Bunnies dreamt that their mother was turning them over in bed. They stirred a little in their sleep, but still they did not wake up.

Mr. McGregor tied up the sack and left it on the wall.

He went to put away the mowing machine.

While he was gone, Mrs. Flopsy Bunny (who had remained at home) came across the field.

She looked suspiciously at the sack and wondered where everybody was?

Then the mouse came out of her jam pot, and Benjamin took the paper bag off his head, and they told the doleful tale.

Benjamin and Flopsy were in despair, they could not undo the string.

But Mrs. Tittlemouse was a resourceful person. She nibbled a hole in the bottom corner of the sack.

The little rabbits were pulled out and pinched to wake them.

Their parents stuffed the empty sack with three rotten vegetable marrows, an old blacking-brush and two decayed turnips.

Then they all hid under a bush and watched for Mr. McGregor.

Mr. McGregor came back and picked up the sack, and carried it off.

He carried it hanging down, as if it were rather heavy.

The Flopsy Bunnies followed at a safe distance.

They watched him go into his house.

And then they crept up to the window to listen.

Mr. McGregor threw down the sack on the stone floor in a way that would have been extremely painful to the Flopsy Bunnies, if they had happened to have been inside it.

They could hear him drag his chair on the flags, and chuckle —

"One, two, three, four, five, six leetle rabbits!" said Mr. McGregor.

"Eh? What's that? What have they been spoiling now?" enquired Mrs. McGregor.

"One, two, three, four, five, six leetle fat rabbits!" repeated Mr. McGregor, counting on his fingers — "one, two, three —"

"Don't you be silly; what do you mean, you silly old man?"

"In the sack! one, two, three, four, five, six!" replied Mr. McGregor.

(The youngest Flopsy Bunny got upon the window-sill.)

Mrs. McGregor took hold of the sack and felt it. She said she could feel six, but they must be *old* rabbits, because they were so hard and all different shapes.

"Not fit to eat; but the skins will do fine to line my old cloak."

"Line your old cloak?" shouted Mr. McGregor — "I shall sell them and buy myself baccy!"

"Rabbit tobacco! I shall skin them and cut off their heads."

Mrs. McGregor untied the sack and put her hand inside.

When she felt the vegetables she became very very angry. She said that Mr. McGregor had "done it a purpose".

And Mr. McGregor was very angry too. One of the rotten marrows came flying through the kitchen window, and hit the youngest Flopsy Bunny.

It was rather hurt.

Then Benjamin and Flopsy thought that it was time to go home.

So Mr. McGregor did not get his tobacco, and Mrs. McGregor did not get her rabbit skins.

But next Christmas Thomasina Tittlemouse got a present of enough rabbit-wool to make herself a cloak and a hood, and a handsome muff and a pair of warm mittens.

The End

From the Flopsy Bunnies

Beatrix Potter often wrote Christmas letters
and cards from her characters to her readers.
These were sent to the son of a friend.

Dear Master
John Hough,

I wish you a Merry
Christmas! I am going
to have an apple for
my Christmas dinner &
some celery tops.
The cabbages are all
frosted but there is
lots of hay.

Yrs. aff.
First Flopsy Bunny.
XXXXXX

Dear Master John,
I wish you the
same as my eldest
brother, and I am
going to have the
same dinner.

Yrs. aff
2ⁿᵈ. Flopsy Bunny.

xxxxxx

Some of the Flopsy Bunnies were better at writing letters than others!

Dear Master Hough,

I wish you the compliments of the Season. We have got new fur tippets for Christmas.

Yrs. aff.

3rd. (Miss) F. Bunny.
XXX

Dear Master John,
I have not learned to rite propperly.

Love from

4th Miss F. Bunny

XXXXX
5th Miss F. Bunny

XXX
with his love,
from the 6th Master F. B.

THE TALE OF
TWO BAD MICE

ABOUT THIS BOOK

The Tale of Two Bad Mice was written at a particularly happy time for Beatrix Potter: she and her editor, Norman Warne, were becoming firm friends, and Beatrix was sometimes included in Warne family celebrations. Norman made a new cage for Beatrix's pet mice, Tom Thumb and Hunca Munca, so that she could more easily draw them for her new book. He had also made a doll's house for his favourite niece, Winifred, which Beatrix used as the model for the doll's house in her book. She kept some of the furniture all her life, and it can still be seen at Hill Top, her first Lakeland home.

The story makes reference to the Christmas tradition of finding coins in stockings, which originates from St. Nicholas, who dates from the fourth century and left coins in the stockings of poor girls who could not afford dowries to marry.

Once upon a time there was a very beautiful doll's-house; it was red brick with white windows, and it had real muslin curtains and a front door and a chimney.

It belonged to two Dolls called Lucinda and Jane; at least it belonged to Lucinda, but she never ordered meals.

Jane was the Cook; but she never did any cooking, because the dinner had been bought ready-made, in a box full of shavings.

There were two red lobsters and a ham, a fish, a pudding, and some pears and oranges.

They would not come off the plates, but they were extremely beautiful.

One morning Lucinda and Jane had gone out for a drive in the doll's perambulator. There was no one in the nursery, and it was very quiet. Presently there was a little scuffling, scratching noise in a corner near the fire-place, where there was a hole under the skirting-board.

Tom Thumb put out his head for a moment, and then popped it in again.

Tom Thumb was a mouse.

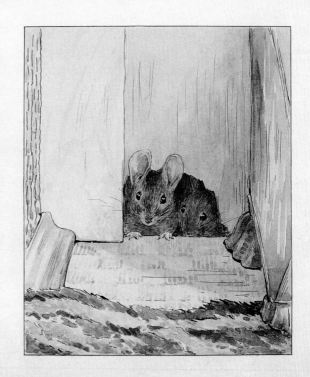

A minute afterwards, Hunca Munca, his wife, put her head out, too; and when she saw that there was no one in the nursery, she ventured out on the oilcloth under the coal-box.

The doll's-house stood at the other side of the fire-place. Tom Thumb and Hunca Munca went cautiously across the hearthrug. They pushed the front door — it was not fast.

Tom Thumb and Hunca Munca went upstairs and peeped into the dining-room. Then they squeaked with joy!

Such a lovely dinner was laid out upon the table! There were tin spoons, and lead knives and forks, and two dolly-chairs — all *so* convenient!

Tom Thumb set to work at once to carve the ham. It was a beautiful shiny yellow, streaked with red.

The knife crumpled up and hurt him; he put his finger in his mouth.

"It is not boiled enough; it is hard. You have a try, Hunca Munca."

Hunca Munca stood up in her chair, and chopped at the ham with another lead knife.

"It's as hard as the hams at the cheesemonger's," said Hunca Munca.

The ham broke off the plate with a jerk, and rolled under the table.

"Let it alone," said Tom Thumb; "give me some fish, Hunca Munca!"

Hunca Munca tried every tin spoon in turn; the fish was glued to the dish.

Then Tom Thumb lost his temper. He put the ham in the middle of the floor, and hit it with the tongs and with the shovel — bang, bang, smash, smash!

The ham flew all into pieces, for underneath the shiny paint it was made of nothing but plaster!

Then there was no end to the rage and disappointment of Tom Thumb and Hunca Munca. They broke up the pudding, the lobsters, the pears and the oranges.

As the fish would not come off the plate, they put it into the red-hot crinkly paper fire in the kitchen; but it would not burn either.

Tom Thumb went up the kitchen chimney and looked out at the top — there was no soot.

While Tom Thumb was up the chimney, Hunca Munca had another disappointment. She found some tiny canisters upon the dresser, labelled — Rice — Coffee — Sago — but when she turned them upside down, there was nothing inside except red and blue beads.

Then those mice set to work to do all the mischief they could — especially Tom Thumb! He took Jane's clothes out of the chest of drawers in her bedroom, and he threw them out of the top floor window.

But Hunca Munca had a frugal mind. After pulling half the feathers out of Lucinda's bolster, she remembered that she herself was in want of a feather bed.

With Tom Thumb's assistance she carried the bolster downstairs, and across the hearthrug. It was difficult to squeeze the bolster into the mouse-hole; but they managed it somehow.

Then Hunca Munca went back and fetched a chair, a book-case, a bird-cage, and several small odds and ends. The book-case and the bird-cage refused to go into the mouse-hole.

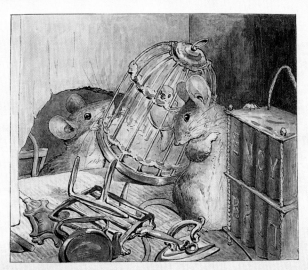

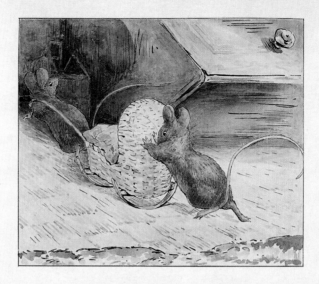

Hunca Munca left them behind the coal-box, and went to fetch a cradle.

Hunca Munca was just returning with another chair, when suddenly there was a noise of talking outside upon the landing. The mice rushed back to their hole, and the dolls came into the nursery.

What a sight met the eyes of Jane and Lucinda!

Lucinda sat upon the upset kitchen stove and stared; and Jane leant against the kitchen dresser and smiled — but neither of them made any remark.

The book-case and the bird-cage were rescued from under the coal-box — but Hunca Munca has got the cradle, and some of Lucinda's clothes.

She also has some useful pots and pans, and several other things.

The little girl that the doll's-house belonged to, said — "I will get a doll dressed like a policeman!"

But the nurse said — "I will set a mouse-trap!"

So that is the story of the two Bad Mice, — but they were not so very very naughty after all, because Tom Thumb paid for everything he broke.

He found a crooked sixpence under the hearthrug; and upon Christmas Eve, he and Hunca Munca stuffed it into one of the stockings of Lucinda and Jane.

And very early every morning — before anybody is awake —
Hunca Munca comes with her dust-pan and her broom to sweep
the Dollies' house!

The End

Christmas Cards

Beatrix Potter had always designed Christmas cards for her friends and family and, from 1890, she produced them for the stationery firm Hildesheiner & Faulkner. Here are a selection of them.

Greetings

A happy New Year to you.

Greetings

A very happy Christmas to you.

A Merry Christmas

A Bright and Happy New Year

Seasons Greetings.

THE RABBITS'
CHRISTMAS PARTY

ABOUT THIS STORY

This sequence of six paintings was done by Beatrix Potter in the early 1890s and shows how a group of rabbits enjoy a traditional Christmas celebration together. Beatrix gave four of the paintings to her aunt, Lucy Roscoe, whose husband, scientist Sir Henry Roscoe, provided Beatrix with valuable help in her natural history studies. The remaining two paintings, showing the rabbits dancing and playing Blind Man's Buff, were a gift to a thirteen-year-old American boy, Henry P. Coolidge, who visited Beatrix in her Lake District home in 1927.

These pictures are recognized as particularly exquisite examples of Beatrix's artistic skill. However, by the time Beatrix gave the final two paintings to the young Henry, she had become somewhat critical of her own work. Around the front paws of one of the rabbits in the third and fourth paintings can be seen the pencil line which Beatrix scribbled directly on to the painting to demonstrate to Henry how wrong she thought the rabbit's anatomy was!

While Beatrix's original paintings did not include any accompanying text, we have here included some very short descriptions to tie the sequence together.

Early in the evening on Christmas Eve, the guests brave the snow
and wind and make their way to the Rabbits' Christmas Party.

After the introductions, a full dinner of winter vegetables and cowslip wine is served. The feast can run to many courses.

Once dinner has been cleared, the dancing begins.
The piper will play waltzes and jigs.

The guests play parlour games late into the night.
Blind Man's Bluff is a particular favourite.

As the evening draws to a close, the guests roast apples around the hearth, sharing festive tales.

At last the party ends and the
guests depart into the cold night.

Merry Christmas!

The End